School

IN THE TIME OF THE

CORONAVIRUS

WRITTEN BY:

Emily Mazzulla, Ph.D.

ILLUSTRATED BY:

Antonija Marinić

To James, Georgia, and Theodore.
Thank you for all of the silver linings.

To Jessica for making this book possible.

For Perry, of course.

School in the Time of the Coronavirus

Published by North Branch Productions, LLC

ISBN 978-1-7354225-0-3 paperback
ISBN 978-1-7354225-2-7 case laminate
ISBN 978-1-7354225-1-0 eBook

Cover Design by:
Chris Treccani
www.3dogcreative.net
Illustrations by:
Antonia Marinić

About the Author

Emily Mazzulla, Ph.D. is a Clinical Psychologist, Clinical Assistant Professor of Psychology at Marquette University (MU) and the MU Director of SWIM Collaboration and Innovation. Dr. Mazzulla's clinical and research interests are in trauma and resilience. She adores spending time with her three children, James, Georgia, and Theodore, and wasting time with her husband, Perry. Dr. Mazzulla lives in Milwaukee, Wisconsin.

"'Happy birthday to you, happy birthday to you, happy birthday dear Maria, happy birthday to you.'
Two times through—twenty seconds. Hands are clean." Maria dried her hands and stared at herself in the mirror. She was worried. "What will it feel like to be back in school after being at home for so long?"

Before the first day, Maria and the other students at Green Brook Elementary School were given a lot of information about changes to expect due to the coronavirus.

Student temperatures will be taken each morning before school.

Students and teachers will wear face masks.

Desks will be six feet apart.

Lunch will be eaten at student desks.

"The adults have thought a lot about new rules
to keep kids safe," Maria's mom said.
Maria listened quietly as she felt her body tense.
She took a sip of water and a deep breath.
"I am not sure about this," Maria said.
"It's all so different."

Maria's mom nodded knowingly as she took her daughter's hand in her own. "It's okay to feel nervous, Maria. You're right, school is going to be different. It will take some time to get used to, but after a while, we will adjust. Let's take this one day at a time, okay?"

Maria had a lot of questions before the first day of school arrived.

"Will I have to wear
a mask all day long?"

"How often
will I wash
my hands?"

Maria and her mom discussed her questions.

"Maria," she said. "I am so glad you are talking to me about what you are feeling and thinking. Let's check in every day after school to see how it is going and make a plan together if we need to."

At first, Maria felt overwhelmed by all of the changes,
but when she started to imagine herself at school,
with her friends, learning and playing, she also felt excited.

"Even though there will be changes this school year, a lot will be the same," she told her mom. "We will still learn and play together, our school colors will still be blue and gold, and our mascot will still be a Wildcat."

The night before the first day, Maria laid out her clothes, packed her backpack, and checked her school supplies. This year, families were given a list of "coronavirus supplies" to go along with the usual list.

• Face mask that covers the mouth and nose. Check.
• Hand sanitizer. Check.
• Disinfectant wipes for desk and locker. Check.
• Tissues. Check.
• Thermometer. Check.

Even though Maria had everything on the list, she still felt uneasy. "What if I don't have what I need or feel worried at school?" Maria asked her mom as she got into bed.

"Well, what did you do last year in those situations?" her mom said.

"I asked a teacher for help," replied Maria.

"That's right. The adults at school are there when you need them and I'll be here at home when you need me."

"Okay," Maria said. "Mom, I am going to miss you when I'm at school. I liked spending so much time with you even though I didn't always like learning from the computer. It made me feel safe."

"My darling, I love spending time with you too.
Let's keep reading our detective books, playing dress up,
and baking together."

"Oh! I can even keep giving you haircuts! I like playing salon!"

"Well," said Maria, "maybe *some* things can go back to the way they were before the coronavirus!"

The next morning was the first day of the new school year. "Maria, it's time to go sweetie," her mom said. "We don't want to be late!" Maria's mother stood by the front door holding Maria's backpack in one hand and her lunch in the other. "Are you ready?" she asked softly.

Maria smiled, took a deep breath,
and nodded. "Yes," she said. "I am ready!"

Maria's mom smiled back and gave her a hug
before they walked to the car.
"It's going to be a great year."

Resilience is the ability to cope under stressful or traumatic circumstances. Using resilience building strategies in challenging times can help your child re-establish a sense of safety and manage the stress they might be feeling. Children are resilient and if given the tools, can thrive in the face of adversity.

Resilience Focused Coping Strategies

1. Validate your child's experiences and emotions. Tell your child that it is okay to feel their feelings and that they are safe.

2. No feeling lasts forever. Both challenging and pleasurable emotions come and go. Remind your child when they are feeling intensely that they won't feel this way forever.

3. Coping techniques that calm the body are helpful in most situations! Deep breathing, grounding with your five senses, relaxation, focusing on the present moment, and taking a break are a few strategies that help settle the body.

4. Distraction techniques such as laughter, exercise, talking with a loved one, reading, singing, dancing, or drawing help to take your child's mind off of the coronavirus and calms the body.

5. Help your child understand that problems have solutions even if the solutions are not obvious. When reading a story or discussing a real-life event, talk to your child about how you and others solve problems. Solutions become clearer when the body is settled.

6. Remind your child that they can do difficult things. Take it one step at a time.

7. Provide support. Let your child know that there are many people who care about them and will help when needed.

8. Keep things in perspective. Even the most difficult times are temporary. Although we do not know exactly when or under what conditions, the impact of the virus will lessen, social distancing will end and you and your child will be able to live the life you value with those you care about.

9. Model these skills for your child in your own life and be compassionate with yourself when you have setbacks.

Made in the USA
Monee, IL
11 October 2020